Disney

Whisker Haven
TALES
with the
palace pets

The Critterzen Clue Contest

By Kathy Ellen Davis

Illustrated by the Disney Storybook Art Team

A Random House PICTUREBACK® Book
Random House 🏠 New York

randomhousekids.com

ISBN 978-0-7364-3593-2

Printed in the United States of America

10 9 8 7 6 5 4 3 2 1

One day, Ms. Featherbon gathered the Palace Pets together for an announcement.

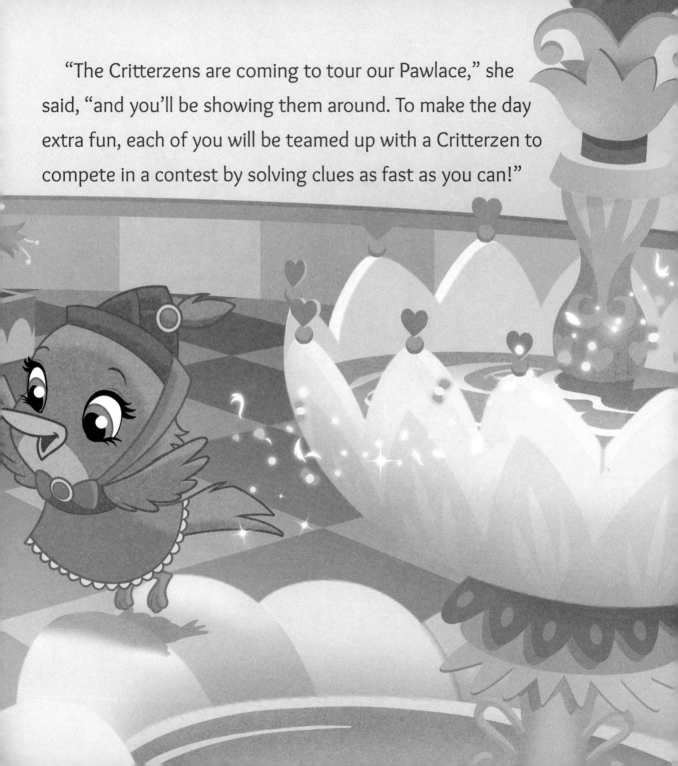

"The Critterzens are coming to tour our Pawlace," she said, "and you'll be showing them around. To make the day extra fun, each of you will be teamed up with a Critterzen to compete in a contest by solving clues as fast as you can!"

Sultan was excited. He loved to **zip** and **zoom**.

My team will win for sure,

he thought.

One by one, the teams were assembled.
Each pet was paired with a Critterzen . . .
except Sultan.

"Where's my partner?" he growled.

Just then, Miss Sophia the sloth casually strolled in. "You will be a perfect teammate for Sultan," said Ms. Featherbon.

Sultan couldn't believe his bad luck. Miss Sofia was the absolute slowest Critterzen.

Ms. Featherbon handed each team a piece of paper. Sultan unrolled his and read it.

Have a peek in here
to reveal your next clue.
Find a book about someone
who's dear to you.

The pets led their Critterzen teammates to Petite's library. Sultan started to panic. "I don't know who's dear to me!" he cried.

Miss Sophia slowly tilted her head. She saw Dreamy grab a copy of *Sleeping Beauty*. And Petite had *Beauty and the Beast*. Miss Sophia knew just what to do.

"Isn't **Princess Jasmine** dear to you?" Miss Sophia asked Sultan as she pulled a copy of *Aladdin* off a shelf. She opened the book and found another clue!

Lucky guess, thought Sultan.

The next clue read:

Visit the pool for
the next leg of our trip.
Bring me a pirate
from the starriest ship.

Sultan took Miss Sophia to Treasure's pool. "How do we know which ship is the starriest?" he whispered.

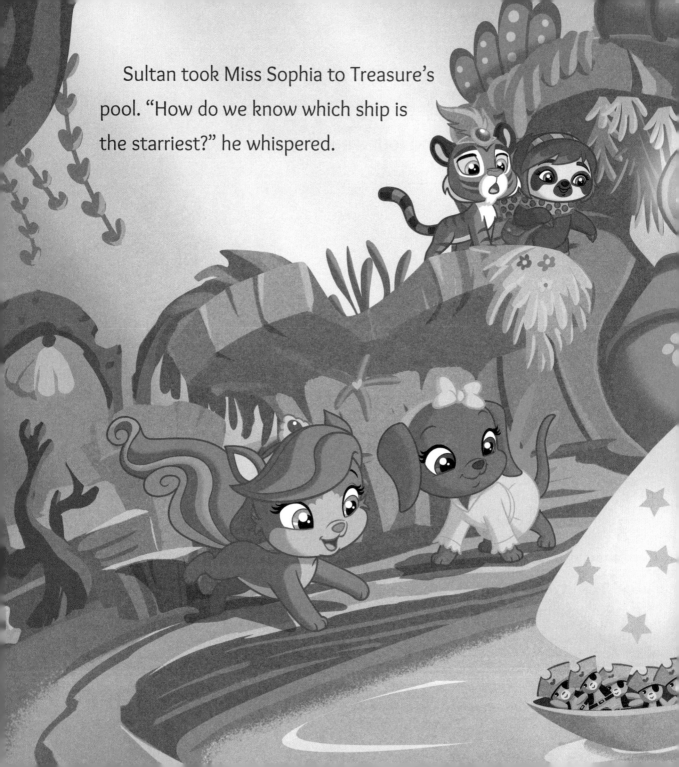

Miss Sophia studied each ship in the pool. "I think . . .
we need to . . . look at the sails," she answered.

Sheesh, thought Sultan. *She even talks slowly.*

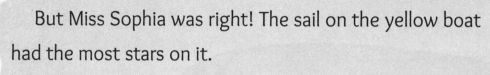

But Miss Sophia was right! The sail on the yellow boat had the most stars on it.

"Leave . . . it . . . to . . . me!" said Miss Sophia. She dove into the water.

Watching his teammate, Sultan thought of a way he could speed things up a bit.

"Hop on!" he said as Miss
ophia swam ashore. "We can go
ster together."

They zipped back to the atrium
trade the pirate for another clue.

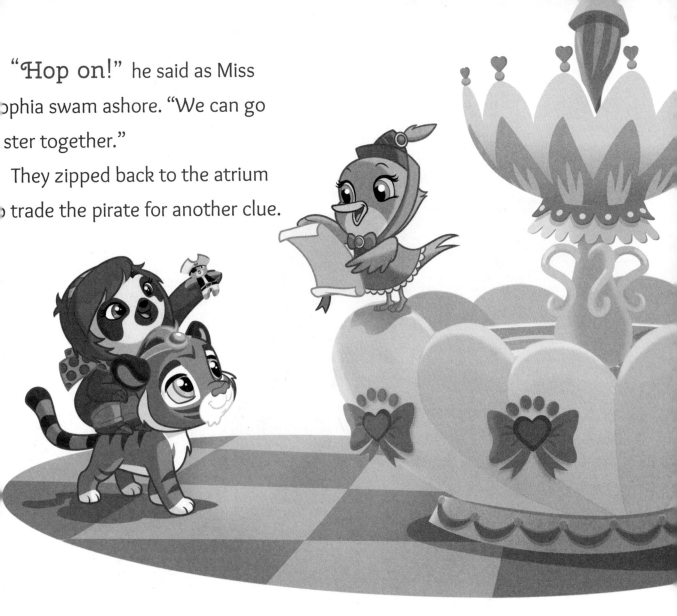

"Excellent job," said Ms. Featherbon. "Your next clue is 'In a gym
ke a jungle, you'll discover a maze. Then return what you find to
y loving gaze.'"

Sultan knew right away that they needed to go to his Jungly Jungle gym. But he was confused when they arrived.

"There's no maze here," he said. "This must be the wrong spot."

"Wait," said Miss Sophia, pausing to nibble on a snack. She pointed to the sparkly trails all around them. "It's a glitter maze!"

They followed the sparkles and found a jar of glitterbits. "You were right again, Miss Sophia!" said Sultan. "Let's take this to Ms. Featherbon."

"Splendificent!" exclaimed Ms. Featherbon. "Your next clue is 'Primping gives Pumpkin so much glee. How many purple objects do you see?'" Thankfully, Sultan knew they had to go . . .

. . . to Pumpkin's primp zone!

Sultan took a quick look around.

"There are seven purple objects!" he shouted.

"But look . . . at the . . . hats," Miss Sophia hispered.

Sultan growled. "None of the hats are purple."

"What . . . about . . . the ribbons?" she asked.

Sultan looked again. Sure enough, Miss Sophia as right. One of the hats had a purple ribbon.

"Eight!" Sultan and Miss Sophia yelled as they reached the atrium.

"Oh, my! And with such gusto!" said Ms. Featherbon. Then she read the last clue: "'Dreamy likes this each night before bed. But don't spill a drop, or she'll stay up instead.'"

Sultan thought for a moment. "I know we cats love milk," he said.

Sultan rushed Miss Sophia into Dreamy's bedroom. He quickly grabbed Dreamy's milk bowl.

"Careful!" Miss Sophia warned. "The clue said . . . we can't spill . . . a drop."

But Sultan was anxious. *Will the other teams catch up?*

Just then, Treasure and Lucy rushed by them, shouting, "We did it!"

Sultan was very disappointed—until he heard Ms. Featherbon say, "I'm sorry, but Dreamy's blanket is not correct."

That meant Sultan and Miss Sophia still had a chance!

"Okay, show me how to go slowly," Sultan said to Miss Sophi

They carefully held the milk bowl. Not a drop spilled!

At the awards ceremony, everyone enjoyed some treats
and congratulated Sultan and Miss Sophia for coming in first.
"We make a great team," Miss Sophia told Sultan.
But the tiger looked at the floor.

"I'm sorry, Miss Sophia," Sultan said. "I thought you'd be a bad partner because you're slow. But you're smart and careful, and we won because of you."

"I'm just happy I won a new friend," Miss Sophia said.

Sultan roared with joy. "Me too!"